ACTION MOVIE
MOVIE

THE PLAY

Action Movie: The Play

ISBN-13: 978-1944540432

For information about production rights, contact:
JoeFoust@hotmail.com

Published by Sordelet Ink
WWW.SORDELETINK.COM

Cover by David Blixt

ACTION MOVIE
THE PLAY

BY
JOE FOUST
AND
RICHARD RAGSDALE

SORDELET
ink

ACTION MOVIE: THE PLAY received its world-premiere production from Defiant Theatre on July 22nd, 1998 at the American Theater Company, directed by Joe Foust. Set design by Martin McClendon, sound design by Gregor Mortis with special audio effects by Greg Nishimura and Sean Sinitski and original music by Prank, lighting design by Richy Norwood, costume design by Jennifer Keller, prop design by Will Shutz, fight direction by Joe Foust and cast, special visual effects by Kirk Anderson, B. Emil Boulos, John De Leonardis, Joe Foust, Andrew Leman, Martin McClarendon, Christopher Thometz, and Jonathan Watkins. Stage management was by Krissy Shields, assisted by Sarah Pace. The cast was as follows:

WILL SCHUTZ -Doctor Xyelene

CHRISTOPHER THOMETZ - Stone Hardgod

LISA ROTHSCHILLER - Cyborg Woman

ED PIERCE - Alec Smarty

CHRISTOPHER JOHNSON - Jack Jackson

JIM SLONINA - Kung Fu Guy

KIRK ANDERSON - John Kreegar

MICHELE DIMASO - Poison Inimann

MICHAEL F. GOLDBERG - Pike Calypso, Bradley's Golfing Buddy

JOEL MEHR - Chaplain, Panel Technician, Dirkson, Jerry, Scantily Clad Front Door Guard

KATI BRAZDA - Mother, Clean Room Technician

CHERISE SILVESTRI/KRISSY SHIELDS/SARAH PACE - Diane, Pregnant Teenager

GEOFF COATES - Clean Room Technician, Lenny, Ridiculously Stupid Front Door Guard

SEAN SINITSKI - Jose, Sanchez' homey, Cuthington, Bradley Rivers

JOHN DE LEONARDIS - Syfan the Eldrich

RICHARD RAGSDALE - Harry, Hojoitz, Head Guard of Propaganda Office, Dealing Front Door Guard

GREGOR MORTIS - Sanchez, Spike

JENNIFER GEHR - Sergeant Flattop

A. BRYAN GUTHRIE - Ki

UNDERSTUDIES: PISUT VONGKASEMSIRI, KRISSY SHIELDS, JONATHAN WATKINS, KEITH ELITS, JULIE GREENBERG, MICHAEL MAZZARA, SARAH PACE, CHRISTOPHER TAYLOR RANTA

CAST OF CHARACTERS

The Team

Doctor Xyelene
Stone Hardgod
Cyborg Woman
Alec Smarty
Jack Jackson
Kung Fu Guy

World Corp

John Kreegar
Poison Inimann
Pike Calypso

In Order of Appearance

Chaplain
Mother
Diane
Panel Technician
Clean Room Technicians
Harry
Pregnant Teenager
Sanchez
Jose, Sanchez' homey
Sergeant Flattop
Dirkson
Hojoitz
Spike
Lenny
Head Guard of Propaganda Office
Cuthington
Jerry
Dealing Front Door Guard
Scantily Clad Front Door Guard
Ridiculously Stupid Front Door Guard
Bradley Rivers
Bradley's Golfing Buddy
Syfan the Eldrich
Guards, Thugs, Extras, Kokens
Ki

A Quick Word from the Authors

We began working on a theater style back in the old Defiant Theatre days that would explore what theater could do better than movies. Concepts like live actual danger and using the audiences' imagination blended with ours. So it's a little ironic that our most successful venture in this style was based on movies.

Some tips for producing this:

• We used kokens, an idea stolen from kabuki theatre. They are dressed in all black and have black cloth hoods that cover their faces. They are aesthetically invisible and can be used to move objects, lift people, or even make a necktie blow in the wind.

• Cheaper and dumber is better. A 2D cutout of an erlenmeyer flask is better than a real one.

• Almost our whole cast also worked on making, designing, painting and brainstorming. it was group play.

• We originally based this on the stereotypes of 80s action films and embracing that in design can be helpful.

• If you want to use actual weapons, as we did, please put a professional fight choreographer on your team. Be safe.

• You can change, add, cut anything you want. This is your time to play. But if we like it more we reserve the right to put it in future versions. Fair is fair.

• Have fun and make each other laugh.

Contact joefoust@hotmail.com for rights to produce. That's right. Hotmail. We are old school as hell.

ACTION MOVIE

VIETNAM 1972

(Sounds of war. Soldiers run through the house. KREEGAR parachutes in. CHAPLAIN attends to a baby. Sound of a Helicopter. KREEGAR tosses parachute away and goes to CHAPLAIN. They speak loudly over the deafening gunfire and sounds of war)

KREEGAR
FATHER! I have to make a confession.

CHAPLAIN
I'm not so sure this is a good time.

KREEGAR
PLEASE! It's really, really important.

(CHAPLAIN motions to two stools. He pulls a shade down, and the sounds of war are completely muted)

KREEGAR
Father, forgive me, for I have sinned.

CHAPLAIN
How long has it been since your last—

KREEGAR
Excuse me, padre, if you don't mind—I'M TRYING TO TELL A STORY HERE! Shh. So rude! I'm private first class John Kreegar. Now, although the soldier's life is obviously below my station, the objectives of the U.S. government just happened to coincide with a certain little... objective of my own...which brings us to today. *(KREEGAR stands and addresses the audience)* The last day of my tour. My platoon was on a search-and-destroy mission in a small Cambodian village, and I was going from hooch to hooch burning children, marking them with playing cards, making necklaces from their ears – pretty typical stuff, really. And I was searching around for ladies under—things to dress the village elder up in, before we chased him around with hotsticks— when, lo and behold, there it was. The object of my...objective! *(to CHAPLAIN)* Now, I don't know if YOU know anything about Southeast Asian archeology...

CHAPLAIN
...As a matter of fact, I...

KREEGAR
...BUT, suffice it to say, I was on the trail of an artifact of incredible power that was obliquely referred to in a number of forbidden texts and only whispered about in the knighted halls of academia. And there it was, in a simple peasant's hut. The fools, they had no idea of its power. They—they were using it as a paperweight. Heh-heh. A PAPERWEIGHT. And now I have it.

(He produces a small object and holds it in the air)
THE PAPERWEIGHT OF SYFAN!

(He olds the artifact high in the air. Musical stinger. Spotlight. Lights return to normal)

KREEGAR
Roughly translated, THE PAPERWEIGHT OF WORLD DOMINATION!

(He holds the artifact higher in the air. Grander musical stinger. Spotlight. Lights return to normal)

KREEGAR
HE WHO HOLDS THE PAPERWEIGHT WILL eventually DOMINATE THE WORLD!

(He holds it high again. The grandest of musical stingers. Spotlight. Lights return to normal. He thrusts the artifact in the air again. Nothing. He emphasizes it one more time to the booth. Nothing. He gives up, and returns to his story)

KREEGAR
Next thing I know, my so-called squad leader, Stone Hardgod, that incompetent boob, shows up and...

CHAPLAIN
You mean the same Stone Hardgod who single handedly won the battle of...

(KREEGAR makes noises so as not to hear)

KREEGAR
He barged in, WITHOUT knocking, and had the unmitigated gall to inform me that it was "time" for "lunch." Well, I cared not for the tone that fat-brained knuckle-dragger used, so I informed him that his boot was untied—*(all sly)* which it wasn't—and when he made to look, I foxed a

grenade into his pants. Sans pin. Well, five seconds and fifty feet later, my confirmed kill count was brought up to an even three hundred sixty-four. Then I toddled off to base camp to catch the last flight OUTTA HERE!

CHAPLAIN
Oh my God.

KREEGAR
(He's all school-girl secrets) I know, I know, I just had to tell somebody.

CHAPLAIN
Oh my God, You mean to say you're personally responsible for the deaths of three hundred sixty-four people?

KREEGAR
Correction. Three sixty-five.

(KREEGAR shoots the CHAPLAIN)

KREEGAR
It's been a very good year.

(The CHAPLAIN dies a long, slow, painful, spectacular death. The baby giggles)

KREEGAR
Oooh, might as well get a jump on next year.

(He picks up the baby and speaks some cutesy baby gibberish until the baby bites him)

KREEGAR
OW!

(He punches the baby several times. As he shakes the baby, the baby starts to cry. He snaps the baby's neck. Enter STONE HARDGOD)

HARDGOD
KREEGAR!

KREEGAR
HARDGOD! What are you doing alive? Uh, I mean, oh my God, you're alive. Give us a hug.

HARDGOD
What in the hell are you doing here?

KREEGAR
(Hiding the baby behind his back) Nothing.

HARDGOD
Explain yourself.

KREEGAR
It was like this when I got here.

HARDGOD
I am not buying your line of shit, Mister.

KREEGAR
No?

HARDGOD
You killed all of them just like you tried to kill me!

KREEGAR
That's not how I remember it.

HARDGOD
You threw a ger-nade into the pants I was awearin'!

KREEGAR
Oh, that. You see, that was...

HARDGOD
Looks like you need a taste of justice—Hardgod style.

KREEGAR
Pounce!

(KREEGAR tosses the baby at HARDGOD who catches it, throws it to the ground, and punches it in the face, then realizes his mistake. A GIRL SCOUT enters)

GIRL SCOUT
Would you like to buy some Girl Scout cookies?

KREEGAR
Oooooh! Cookies! What'd'ya say, Hardgod? If we discuss this reasonably over a delicious Thin Mint cookie. I'm sure we can come to some sort of...

(KREEGAR grabs the GIRL SCOUT and puts a gun to her head)

KREEGAR
Drop the gun, shitbird, or Twinkie here makes a farm purchase.

(HARDGOD puts his gun down)

KREEGAR
You see, that's your problem Hardgod. You've got a soft heart to match your soft head.

(KREEGAR shoots HARDGOD. HARDGOD falls to the ground. KREEGAR swings the GIRL SCOUT around and shoots her dead)

KREEGAR
Well, it's not like I was gonna pay for those cookies. For you see, I'm evil. *(Maniacal giggle. He snatches the cookies. Maniacal chortle)* Now if you will excuse me, I believe I have a world to dominate. *(Maniacal guffaw. He turns to exit, and sees the shade)* I'm taking this, too. *(With a maniacal*

*cackle, he snatches the shade, and runs off. A heli-
copter carries him away. The lights begin to fade)*

HARDGOD
(voice over) I was dying, but death wasn't an
option. I had too much on my mind. As I laid
there, spilling my blood into the ground, I could
only think of one thing. *(Pause)* Revenge.

(Transition to:)

OPENING CREDITS

*(Oh, yes, opening credits: a smash cut montage of
various action sequences accompanied by show credits of the cast and crew. Transition to:)*

A CITY SIDEWALK

*(There is a World Corp. poster featuring
KREEGAR. HARDGOD, now a homeless bum,
enters with a shopping cart. Two WORLD CORP
GUARDS cross the stage with a couple in their
pajamas)*

GUARDS
Get moving! You talk, I shoot. *(etc.)*

*(After the GUARDS have left, HARDGOD
approaches the World Corp poster and spits on it.
Enter DR. XYLENE, a bald be-goggled man in a
high-tech wheelchair who speaks with a German
accent. He carries a briefcase)*

XYLENE
Looks like you have some pretty strong feelings
about our Mr. Kreegar.

HARDGOD
Eat sand, cripple.

XYLENE
STONE!

(Pause)

HARDGOD
Nobody's called me that in years.

XYLENE
Allow me to introduce myself. My name is Dr. Xylene. I know all about what Kreegar did to you in Vietnam. A man of my wealth has his resources. *(XYLENE opens the briefcase, revealing that it is full of cash, even inside the lid, then slams it shut)* I'm taking action against our Mr. Kreegar. If someone doesn't stop World Corp now, it will be too late. In two weeks time, Kreegar will complete his "World Merge" project. After that, he'll be unstoppable. His every whim will be the screaming agony of the masses.

HARDGOD
That's some pretty straightforward exposition there, baldy.

XYLENE
Why, thank you. By the way, I would prefer you call me Dr. Xylene.

HARDGOD
Whatever you say, baldy.

XYLENE
(Sputters, then...) Look, Stone. I need your help. Can I count on you?

HARDGOD
There's only two things in this world you can count on. An abacus, and Stone Hardgod. But,

uh, how do you figure some old bum and a rich cripple stand a chance against a man like Kreegar?

XYLENE
Oh, we won't be working alone.
They nod slowly and knowingly in agreement.

(Transition to the inside of KREEGAR's Public Headquarters. Sound: "Intruder Alert!" We hear a female computer voice)

COMPUTER
Observation deck.

(Star Trek door-opening sound. Enter CYBORG-WOMAN, she is half-steel, half muscle and all woman. Near the upstage ladder is one of those coin-operated tourist binoculars you might see at the Empire State Building. Four GUARDS rush on, closely followed by POISON INNIMAN, a leather-clad bodyguard that looks CYBORG WOMAN's match in more ways than one. Big fight, POISON left standing)

POISON
Well, well, well. Cyborg Woman. What's a nice girl like you doing in a place like this? Shouldn't you be out cleaning the Jetson's house?

CYBORG WOMAN
Shouldn't you be putting Neosporin on your "property of Kreegar" tattoo?

POISON
Kreegar doesn't tell me what to do. Kreegar pays me to do what I enjoy, which includes killing you.

(POISON pulls gun. CYBORG grabs a guard, using him as a human shield)

POISON
Now, I can't have you holding one of my men hostage.

CYBORG WOMAN
You don't have a choice.

(POISON shoots the guard, and he slumps to the floor)

GUARD
(betrayed) HEY!

CYBORG WOMAN
Okay... *(She rushes up the upstage ladder)*

(POISON, although only four feet away from her, rushes to the binoculars, inserts a coin, and looks up at CYBORG WOMAN climbing the ladder)

POISON
(Turns back to unseen forces) She's heading up to the roof. I call dibs. *(Runs up the ladder)*

(On an adjacent building, HARDGOD and XYLENE are observing the fight)

HARDGOD
(With binoculars) Do you think she needs our help?

XYLENE
Oh, no. Not Cyborg Woman. She can handle herself. She was the highest paid bounty hunter in the Western Hemisphere, until Kreegar set her up for a crime she didn't commit. A few years back, Kreegar's security forces got the drop on her and left her for dead. Little did they know... When she finally did resurface, sixty percent of her body had been replaced with Solid State®

micro-circuitry and a super-light titanium alumi-num alloy. A records check revealed that this drained her formerly considerable Swiss bank account, making her a perfect candidate for our little project. Money aside... *(Displays briefcase full of money)*...where Kreegar is concerned, she would welcome any chance to piss on his parade.

HARDGOD
Yep, she's got a nice set of tatas, all right.

(A pause of bewilderment)

XYLENE
The other one's Poison Inimann, Kreegar's personal bodyguard, a lesbian with a—

HARDGOD
Look, I've about had it about up to here with your exposition, there, baldy. Jeez.

XYLENE
(Hurt) Fine. And I was just about to tell you that you clean up real good.

HARDGOD
What, this old thing? I didn't I was gonna fit in the pants this year...*(as an apology)* Oh, and, uh, Xylene – you've got a nice set of tatas, too.

(HARDGOD returns to his binoculars while XYLENE indicates his embarrassment. Indication is critical to good acting. Transition to:)

WORLD CORP DOWNTOWN ROOFTOP

(We see a bird's eye view of CYBORG WOMAN hanging from the side of the building. POISON is looking down at her)

POISON
Poor darling. What made you think you'd find
Kreegar at his public headquarters, silly bunny?
(Viciously stomps on CYBORG WOMAN's hand)
He's safe where you'll never find him. But I'll
make you deal – if you promise to hold my hand
at the movies, I'll let you up. No? *(Another vicious
stomp)*

*(A baby buggy appears. Crying. POISON grabs the
baby and swings it over her head.*

POISON
Don't let the precious baby fall!

*(POISON tosses the baby. CYBORG WOMAN
catches the baby. A MOTHER pops out of a building window)*

MOTHER
OH MY GOD MY BABY! NO!

*(CYBORG WOMAN gives the baby to the
MOTHER)*

MOTHER
THANK YOUTHANK YOU! *(Smacks baby)*
Bad baby! *(Exit MOTHER)*

POISON
It's a shame we didn't get to know each other
better, but every time I use a Solid State micro-
circuit, I'll think of you.

*(Cue the Bionic Woman sound. CYBORG
WOMAN grabs POISON's leg, and in a clas-
sic Peckinpah slow motion sequence, POISON
ends up hanging from the building with CYBORG
WOMAN looking down)*

CYBORG WOMAN
Well, see ya.

(HARDGOD and XYLENE are revealed)

POISON
Aren't going to say, "Hang in there"? "You have so many hang-ups"? HEY! Don't just leave me here.

HARDGOD
That's some pretty good work there, missy.

CYBORG WOMAN
I'm no missy, and you're no man.

POISON
How about, "Now that's what I call hanging someone out to dry"?

XYLENE
Cyborg Woman, we have a proposition for you. *(Opens briefcase full of money)* We're going after Kreegar.

CYBORG WOMAN
Well, you boys sure do know how to treat a lady. But how do you think the three of us stand a chance against a man like Kreegar?

XYLENE
Oh, we won't be working alone.

(CYBORG WOMAN, HARDGOD, and XYLENE all nod slowly in agreement)

POISON
How about, "Now that's what I call a well hung bodyguard"?

CYBORG WOMAN
SHUT UP!

(Transition to:)

WORLD CORP SCIENTIFIC LABORATORY

(ALEC SMARTY sits at a computer. Two TECHNICIANS [one is DIANE] are at a panel. Two other TECHNICIANS are in a clean room performing malicious experiments with a hamster)

PANEL TECHNICIAN
Hey, Alec, did you finish those algorithms?

SMARTY
Are we still pretending I know what an algorithm is!? If they're anything like Swiss cake rolls, then yes, I finished them. Hours ago.

DIANE
Alec Smarty, how can you pretend to not know what algorithms are? You wrote most of the auto-mated reasoning code that runs this facility.

SMARTY
Oh, do you mean the process or set of rules to be followed in calculations or other problem-solving operations? Then why don't you guys just say that? You NPR-way-with-words nerds! Algorithms? I mean really.

(In the clean room, an Erlenmeyer flask is dropped. A blaring emergency alarm. One TECHNICIAN sprints from the clean room toward SMARTY, suddenly turns back, grabs a quick drink from the water fountain that is merely a 2-D painting on the lab set, and rushes to SMARTY)

CLEAN ROOM TECH
Sir! Virus #17 has escaped!

SMARTY
(Standing) Oh my God, that's the funky shit!

(Music and big dance number. Eventually, SMARTY works his way to his desk, puts on earmuffs and places a garbage pail over his head. His colleagues dance him over to the panic button, which is pressed with SMARTY's head. The lights return to normal, and everyone is exhausted. DIANE and PANEL TECHNICIAN exit)

CLEAN ROOM TECH
Wait a minute. You mean to tell me I'm supposed to believe in a virus that makes me dance?

SMARTY
You invented it.

CLEAN ROOM TECH.
Right!

SMARTY
(Sarcastically to other techs) Probably using algorithms!

(The CLEAN ROOM TECHNICIAN exits as XYLENE and HARDGOD enter)

XYLENE
An excellent display of quick thinking, Mr. Smarty.

SMARTY
Thank you, thank you. Don't get up. The trashcan was the key, and the ear muffs were the icing on the WAIT A MINUTE! How did you two get in here? This is a "restricted area." *(Indicating sign that reads the same)*

XYLENE
We have a proposition for you. We are going after
John Kreegar.

SMARTY
John Kreegar? *(Puts on earmuffs)* I can't hear you!
La la la la la la...

HARDGOD
Hey! *(Pulls the earmuffs from SMARTY's head)*
You know what Kreegar's doing to this world.

*(Meanwhile, the PANEL TECHNICIAN enters.
He runs the water at the 2-D drinking fountain
for the water to get cold before taking his drink)*

XYLENE
And to you. Downsizing your team. Slashing
your salary. Patenting all of your ideas. Cutting
all benefits. Installing cameras in your home.
Retaining all rights to your body after you
die? My God, man! Kreegar is processing the
remains of deceased employees into luncheon
meat which is then sold in the company cafete-
ria!

*(PANEL TECHNICIAN, just about to bite into
his sandwich, stops short. Then shrugs, sprinkles
on some hot sauce and tucks in while exiting. For
extra fun, if you have a rubber hand lying around,
you can use that for the sandwich filling)*

HARDGOD
The way I see it, you've got two choices. You can
either sit on your ASS and let Kreegar take over
the world. Or, you can get out there and fight for
everything you hold dear in this world. *(Salutes)*
GEH!

SMARTY
Gosh. When you put it like that, it really clears things up for me. Somebody got a pillow for my ASS!?

(CYBORG WOMAN enters with briefcase full of money and drops it on the floor in front of SMARTY)

SMARTY
That'll do. *(As SMARTY bends down, he catches his reflection in CYBORG WOMAN's steel panties)* Wow, I can sure see myself in your pants.

(SMARTY receives an eye poke from CYBORG WOMAN)

CYBORG
Now you can't.

SMARTY
Ow? What was that about? I was merely commenting on the reflecting surface... Oh, I see. It sounds like the other thing.

XYLENE
Enough of this. The clock is our enemy, and our team is not yet complete. *(XYLENE, HARDGOD, and CYBORG WOMAN exit)*

SMARTY
My eyes! I can't see my eyes! Oh, hey guys, wait up.

(DIANE enters. SMARTY, following the rest of his team, swings back around, grabs money, and approaches DIANE)

SMARTY
Hey, Diane—guess who can afford to move out of

his parents' basement?

(HARDGOD enters and drags SMARTY out)

SMARTY
I'll call you!

(They exit. Transition to:)

AN INNER CITY STREET

(HARRY and JACK JACKSON on stakeout. Police radio is heard in background. HARRY is seated in the passenger seat and JACKSON in the driver's seat. Harry is drinking coffee, JACKSON with binoculars)

JACKSON
Jack Jackson reporting in. No sign of Sanchez. Over.

(Long pause)

HARRY
I hate stakeouts. They're so tedious. How long we been here?

(JACKSON does a watch take)

JACKSON
About forty-five minutes.

(Pause)

HARRY
JESUS! WILL IT NEVER END? Last day on the force, and I've got to pull stakeout. One day away from retirement. You know, tomorrow I'm gonna take my retarded son to Disneyland. I can say retarded. I'm the father. Right after renewing my wedding vows. Twenty years we've been together,

the wife and I. Stop and pick up Mom at the hospital – they say she's fine—pay off the mortgage and buy that ranch in Montana the wife and I are always talking about, and breed unicorns.

JACKSON
Yup, you've got a lot to live for.

HARRY
And a lot to be proud of. You know, Jackson, we're the last true cops this town will know. In less than three years, World Corp will have phased out city police all together. Then Kreegar's security force will run the whole show.

JACKSON
Why are you always telling me stuff I already know?

HARRY
Beats me. What time is it?

JACKSON
Noon.

HARRY
Lunch!

(They take out their doughnut sandwiches and begin to eat. A PREGNANT TEENAGER enters pulling a needle out of her arm. HARRY notices her first. He does a spit take all over JACKSON)

HARRY
Hey look!

JACKSON
What?

PREGNANT TEENAGER
Wow! What a rush! *(Speaking to her pregnant belly)* Goo, goo, goo. You feel that baby? *(To JACKSON)* Thanks Sanchez! *(She reaches out and falls over dead)*

JACKSON
Sanchez!

(HARRY and JACKSON leap out of the car and rush to the dying PREGNANT TEENAGER. JACKSON checks her breathing)

HARRY
Jackson, she's dead!

Jackson
CPR!

(JACKSON then proceeds to administer a brutal CPR resuscitation maneuver that he has learned on the mean streets. He delivers three solid thrusts with his fists together on the PREGNANT TEENAGER's abdomen. Her body flails with each blow. JACKSON then blows a lung full of air down her throat. Checks her. Nothing. Listens to her chest. Nothing. Shakes her belly. Nothing. Listens to her belly. Nothing)

JACKSON
Ugh! *(Slaps hands on ground)* She got all goofed up on smack-balls and OD'd. When will these young, pregnant kids learn that the drug expressway *(punches her stomach for emphasis)* is a dusty back road *(punch)* full of potholes *(punch)* and nuisance speed bumps *(punch)* leading straight to No-wheres-ville! Drugs don't make you cool or popular, they

just make you forget all your troubles and feel
REAL GOOD! When? WHEN!?

*(JACKSON crosses downstage of the PREGNANT
TEENAGER, stepping on her belly)*

JACKSON
Damn you Sanchez! Damn you to hell!

HARRY
Look! There goes Sanchez! Let's roll Jackson!

JACKSON
Check!

*(They leap into the squad car and peel out
Flintstones style, doing about ¼ mph. HARRY
slams on the breaks. JACKSON leaps out of the
car, rushes over to the PREGNANT TEENAGER
and standing over the body with one foot on her
belly, points to the horizon)*

JACKSON
I swear you'll be brought to justice... *(Kicks body)*
SANCHEZ!!!

*(JACKSON rushes back over to the car and gets
in. They peel out and HARRY makes a turn-
ing left-hand signal. He then steps on the breaks
again, JACKSON leaps out and rushes over to the
PREGNANT TEENAGER, straddles her, smacks
her as hard as he can across the face to make sure
she is really dead. He waits. She does not respond.
He waits a few more seconds just to be sure)*

JACKSON
DAMN! *(Rushes back to the car and they resume
pursuit of SANCHEZ and his driver JOSE)*

THE CAR CHASE

(Busy street. Enter SANCHEZ car: a souped up, tricked-out, low rider. The cop car pulls up along side of the SANCHEZ car; HARRY draws his weapon and aims it at Sanchez's car)

HARRY
Police! Pull over!

SANCHEZ
(Mockingly) Oooh, look! It's the police!

(JOSE spins the wheel, taking their car in tight with the cop car. Caught unawares, HARRY with arm still extended is brought up close to SANCHEZ who takes the gun away with a simple wrist slap. HARRY pulls his arm away. And the SANCHEZ low-rider veers away from the cop car)

SANCHEZ
You call that a gun? I'll show you a real gun, pendejo! *(He produces a large, legally purchased, assault weapon and points it at HARRY)* Eat this!

(HARRY pulls the same maneuver that JOSE and SANCHEZ pulled on him, slaps SANCHEZ's wrist, and takes his gun away)

SANCHEZ
Hey! He took my Uzi, man! Give it back!

(The cars pull apart to a safer distance once again. JACKSON opens his door and leans out on the roof of the car, weapon drawn, tie flapping in the breeze. He fires several shots at the SANCHEZ car. JACKSON then gets up onto the roof, and SANCHEZ breaks out the rear window and gets on top of his roof. SANCHEZ and JACKSON

exchange blows, a kick, and then get locked in a deadly game of Roman knuckles. At first, SANCHEZ is winning and then JACKSON gets the upper hand (or knuckle). SANCHEZ grabs JACKSON's package with a disgusting "splat." JACKSON grabs SANCHEZ's head and thrusts it down onto the roof of JACKSON's car. SANCHEZ is now laid out between the two cars, and they move apart, leaving SANCHEZ precariously hanging on by his fingers and toes. JACKSON surveys and walks over the human SANCHEZ bridge to the SANCHEZ car. JOSE now realizes that his boss is in a very bad position. While his guard is down, JACKSON leans over and peers in the driver's window)

JACKSON
Hey!

JOSE
What?

(JOSE looks over and meets JACKSON's fist. Stunned, JOSE looks on as JACKSON, leaning in through the window, takes control of the wheel. JOSE, regaining his senses begins to fight JACKSON for the wheel. The cars are veering out of control. SANCHEZ pulls himself onto the cop car and punches HARRY. They regain their footing, SANCHEZ on the cop hood and JACKSON on the SANCHEZ roof)

SANCHEZ
Get off my car!

JACKSON
Get off MY car!

(SANCHEZ leaps to the hood of his car, punches JACKSON, who recoils)

JACKSON
Ouch!

SANCHEZ
AAAHHHHHHHHHH!

(SANCHEZ is hanging on for his life, regains footing, breaks the windshield. JACKSON leaps back to the roof of the cop car, and SANCHEZ takes position on the roof of his car)

JACKSON
It would be in your best interest to pull over.

SANCHEZ
It would be in your best interest to kiss my aaaaaaaaaaaaaaaaaaaa!

(SANCHEZ looks out in front of the car, Jackson looks to see what is there, JOSE sees it and screams, as does HARRY. The cars swerve apart to narrowly miss colliding with a tree. They swerve back into each other and collide with a smack, then swerve to the left in unison and run onto the sidewalk, heading straight for a PARKING ENFORCEMENT OFFICER who is giving out parking tickets. The P.E. OFFICER is thrown onto the roof of the SANCHEZ car as the cars swerve right, avoiding a FRUIT CART)

ALL
Aaaahhh!

(The cars swerve left, avoiding a BICYCLIST. SANCHEZ punches the OFFICER, and his head is thrown back into the grill of the car, only his feet

jammed up under the roof keep him from becoming road kill as his head grazes the speeding road underneath. The OFFICER regains a footing and fights to get off the SANCHEZ car and onto the hood of the cop car. The cars pull apart again to avoid hitting a construction worker in the road. They swerve back into each other as the OFFICER stands up, straddling the cars with each foot. The cars pull apart leaving him spread eagle. At this point, the OFFICER is hit in the ass by several parking meters as the cop car is being forced to drive on the sidewalk)

SANCHEZ
Get off my car!

(JACKSON gives him a hand and pulls him over to the cop car, but not before SANCHEZ can get in a good nostril pull. The OFFICER is now standing on the roof of the cop car, sure now of his safety. He raised his arms in triumphant glee, unaware of the approaching bridge. The OFFICER get wrapped around the "low clearance" sign that passed over the car and is gone. SANCHEZ and JACKSON exchange glances and call down to the cars)

SANCHEZ / JACKSON
Chainsaw!

(They are handed chainsaws and chainsaw fight time. At some point, JACKSON is bearing down on SANCHEZ, who takes JACKSON's tie and forces it into JACKSON's chainsaw motor, thus giving him a slow strangle)

JACKSON
JESUS!

(JACKSON pulls his tie off, then produces another tie pre-tied around his neck from under his shirt. He gives the audience a double thumbs up and continues to fight with SANCHEZ who loses his saw. On his back, SANCHEZ kicks JACKSON who loses his saw. Both SANCHEZ and JACKSON lean in through the car windows)

JACKSON / SANCHEZ
Gun!

(JOSE hands off a gun to SANCHEZ who shoots upside down through his own car, winging HARRY)

JACKSON
Harry!

(JACKSON leaps onto the hood of the SANCHEZ car and unloads his clip into the engine block. JOSE leaps from the car, JACKSON flips back to the safety of his car, and the SANCHEZ car veers out of control, flips and crashes. SANCHEZ lies unconscious; JACKSON helps the wounded HARRY out of the car and onto the ground)

HARRY
I never thought it would end like this.

JACKSON
That's crazy talk partner. Squirrelly, silly talk.

HARRY
Don't molly-coddle me Jackson! This looks like good-bye. Do two things for me pal?

JACKSON
Sure thing, buddy!

HARRY
Tell my wife I love her.

JACKSON
You got it, Ralph!

HARRY
I'm Harry. Ralph was your third partner.

JACKSON
No, no. Ralph was my eighth partner?

HARRY
That was Jimmy.

JACKSON
Then who the hell is Miles?

HARRY
That's your hairdresser.

JACKSON
Oh, yeah. He died too.
HARRY
Listen! The second thing...

JACKSON
Yeah?

HARRY
Get Sanchez! Avenge me!

JACKSON
OK!

*(JACKSON drops HARRY, who "dies."
SANCHEZ comes to, and crawls out of the wreck-
age of his car. He lights up a cigarette and inhales)*

SANCHEZ
My car!

(JACKSON gets his gun from the roof of the cruiser...)

JACKSON
Hey.

(SANCHEZ spins. JACKSON shoots. SANCHEZ falls to the ground and exhales the smoke. JACKSON approaches, checks the body. Stops and considers if he has done everything. Does a mental checklist and concludes that things are all wrapped up and exits)

HARRY
(Coming to, in a spotlight) Everything's getting dark. I'm scared. Hold my hand Jackson. Jackson. Jackson? *(Sound of a bird screeching)* Is that you Jackson?

(Cue VULTURE that swoops down on poor HARRY and dines)

HARRY
Oww! Please, no. *(Lights fade slowly, transitioning to:)*

INTERIOR OF A POLICE STATION

(JACKSON enters and notices a flashing button. He removes his sunglasses, winces, and presses it reluctantly. A window shaped like a video screen reveals SERGEANT FLATTOP, a Mike Ditka-type, played by a woman in drag)

FLATTOP
Alright, listen up, carpet-munchers. Here's today's agenda. Jackson—that was a sloppy-ass job to did on Sanchez, but at least you took him down. We apprehended his partner, and he'll be appearing

before a judge next week.

JACKSON
Yep. He'll be raping his next victim behind bars.

FLATTOP
I should hope so. Now how about a moment of silence for Jack's old partner.

JACKSON
(Standing) I'm gonna miss you, Ralph.

FLATTOP
Harry.

JACKSON
Harry.

(Moment of silence, broken by FLATTOP)

FLATTOP
Alright, who queefed? *(To an officer OS)* Fuck you, fuckwad. I'll fuck you. Show some respect for a dead motherfucker.

(JACKSON sits)

FLATTOP
Johnson, Dirkson—you're on the Hillson bust.

DIRKSON (OS)
Hey, Sarge, do we get any backup?

FLATTOP
Backup!? Whaddeya squat to pee? Jesus. Go back to the quiltin' bee and say hello to Evelyn for me.

DIRKSON (OS)
Ooh, isn't she the one who always wears that blue dress?

FLATTOP
Shut your hole, puke! Gutierrez, Hojoitz—I'm assigning you to the witness protection program. You're gonna be watching a Miss Bubbles LaRue.

HOJOITZ(OS)
Oh, now, isn't she the one the mafia wants for stooling on that dirty squeal pigeon?

FLATTOP
Mafia? Hey, grandma—knit me a fucking scarf and tie it around my dick SO I CAN COCKSLAP YOU! I know you've got a set of balls, at home, in a box, under your bed. So strap 'em on, and DO YOUR FUCKING JOB! And, Jackson—I've got a special treat just for you. Vest check! *(FLATTOP shoots JACKSON in the chest)*

JACKSON
Ow!

FLATTOP
Vest seems to be working fine. And I've got another treat for you. It's an undercover assignment outside the department, so mind your fucking manners, fuckface. You'll be reporting to a Dr. Xylene.

JACKSON
What's this all about, Sarge?

FLATTOP
Whaddeya want more exposition? Talk to Xylene. *(Indicating audience)* These people've heard it already.

(JACKSON is confused—to whom is the SERGEANT referring?)

FLATTOP
And jackass, do yourself a favor. When you're out there and you get shot—AND YOU WILL!—make sure you're wearin' some clean panties.

(JACKSON gives him a thumbs-up)

FLATTOP
Toodles.

(The video screen window closes, and JACKSON strikes a macho pose. Transition to:)

KUNG FU GUY'S HABERDASHERY

(KUNG FU GUY cleans a hat with exquisite beauty and skill. A gang of hooligans, led by SPIKE, passes by the window and sees the action. KUNG FU GUY completes his hat trick/cleaning)

KUNG FU GUY
Hi.

(He bows. Gong. The gang enters)

SPIKE
Hey, old man. Nice place you got here. Lots of hats.

KUNG FU GUY
I have many hats. Some are beautiful. Some are deadly. But all are clean.

(Gong)

SPIKE
Right. *(Cuckoo whistle)* Listen, old man, my associates and I—we're new to the neighborhood, and we couldn't help but notice that the place is a

PIT. So, we've taken it upon ourselves to help you clean it up a bit. But this kind of work doesn't come for free. Oh, no. That's why we're canvassing the neighborhood looking for...donations. Heh? So we'll be by once a month for your generous tithe. Ha. Whaddya say, old man, huh?

KUNG FU GUY
Not interested.

SPIKE
What?! Lenny, did I hear him right?

LENNY
What'd he say?

SPIKE
"Not interested."

LENNY
Naaaaaaaaaah. YOU didn't hear him right.

SPIKE
I didn't think so.

(SPIKE motions to another gang member and they move in to either side of KUNG FU GUY)

SPIKE
Let me make things clear, old man. You ain't got a choice! You either pony up the dough...or we take your hats.

(KUNG FU GUY remains stone-faced)

SPIKE
Take his hats.

(The other gang member moves to do so, but KUNG FU GUY effortlessly flips him to the ground)

SPIKE
KICK HIS ASS!

(The gang attacks KUNG FU GUY)

KUNG FU GUY
Not effective.

(KUNG FU GUY beats up everyone except for SPIKE. The gang runs off)

SPIKE
Hey, hey, hey—what are you? Chickenshit?

LENNY (OS)
Costume change!

SPIKE
Oh, right. Now you've gotta take on me. WAAAAHH!

(They fight. KUNG FU GUY grabs SPIKES face, and reels his closed hand back with thumb exposed)

KUNG FU GUY
Your nose!

(SPIKE yelps. KUNG FU GUY opens his hand, revealing nothing)

SPIKE
Huh?

(KUNG FU GUY smacks SPIKE flat in the forehead. Much flipping ensues. Some kicks. A 360 degree Matrix effect. KUNG FU GUY tickles SPIKE's foot)

SPIKE
That tickles!

(More fighting. SPIKE grabs a shovel)

SPIKE
Dig this, old man!

(SPIKE swings, and KUNG FU GUY flips him over by the shovel and pulls SPIKE up by his hair)

SPIKE
Ow! Sorry, sorry! Not my hair! OW!

(KUNG FU GUY rips out SPIKE's heart then places a lovely pillbox hat on SPIKE's head. KUNG FU GUY dusts off his hands and turns to the audience)

KUNG FU GUY
Hi.

(He bows. Gong. XYLENE, JACKSON, HARDGOD, SMARTY and CYBORG WOMAN enter from the back door)

HARDGOD
Now that's what I call beating up a guy and putting a hat on his head!

CYBORG WOMAN
Yeah, me too.

XYLENE
Listen. Kung Fu Guy. We have a proposition for you. *(Opens the briefcase full of money)*

KUNG FU GUY
Not interested.

XYLENE
Kreegar has the Paperweight of Syfan.

(Oriental music. Lighting change. KUNG FU GUY

produces a sword and performs a mie of incredible beauty. The lighting returns to normal. SMARTY approaches him)

SMARTY
Hey, how much for this hat that says "heteroflexible"?

(They exit. Transition to:)

INSIDE A WORLD CORP OFFICE

GUARD 1
(Sticking a finger in his ear) Sir, we have a situation here. A disgruntled former employee has taken the Vice President in charge of Propaganda hostage. He's demanding to see Mr. Kreegar and make him "pay for his crimes," or so he says....Yes sir.... Hold tight.... Roger.

(Three more GUARDS enter)

JERRY(OS)
Get out of the way, I said!

(JERRY, an unassuming sadsack, enters with a gun to CUTHINGTON's head)

JERRY
God! Just stand back...stand back or I'll kill him! I'm a serious as a heart attack here. *(Sob)*

(PIKE CALYPSO enters)

PIKE
All right everyone calm down. Men put those guns down.

GUARD 1
But sir!?

PIKE
I said put those guns down. Your name is Jerry, right?

JERRY
Yeah.

PIKE
I remember you from the mailroom, Jerry. You did a damn fine job. Hey, Jerry, look—I know you've got a beef with Kreegar, hell we all do, don't we? But your beef isn't with Cuthington here. Hell Jerry, he's got a wife, two kids and a step-dog who love him very much. So why don't you put the gun down, Jerry? I'm sure we can work something out. Yeah. I don't want anyone to get hurt. *(To GUARD 1)* Take the shot.

GUARD 1
What?

PIKE
Take the fucking shot.

(JERRY overhears and shoots CUTHINGTON dead. JERRY panics)

JERRY
I didn't mean to...

PIKE
Jerry, Jerry, shh, shh...

(PIKE takes JERRY by the arm and embraces him and then proceeds to bite his ear off. PIKE viciously beats JERRY to death, then turns on GUARD 1)

PIKE
Congratulations, deputy dog! You just got your

boss killed! Next time I say take the shot, you take the fucking shot! Now unless you want to find yourself in the Latrine Processing Center, separating shit from corn to make tortillas to eat your poo-poo chalupes, you'll do as I say, No questions asked. Do you understand?!

GUARD 1
(Meekly) Yes, sir.

PIKE
(Chipper) Good. Whoo!

(PIKE walks up to the body of CUTHINGTON and checks it for signs of life by placing his boot on the side of the throat and watching the blood gurgle out onto his boot)

PIKE
(Tasting the blood) AB.

GUARD 1
Huh.

PIKE
(Sniffs) Negative.

GUARD 1
I'll be darned.

PIKE
Well, call an ambulance. Insurance loves that shit. Oh, and ladies? The number is 9-1-1.

GUARD 2
Hut!

(GUARDS exit. PIKE CALYPSO walks through the upstage window and starts spinning in place. Lights go down everywhere but in the window. We

hear the clacking of computer keys. Lights up to reveal
DR XYLENE at a computer with the rest of the
team watching the window as if PIKE CALYPSO's
image is rotating in an enormous computer screen)

XYLENE
Pike Calypso. Head of security at Kreegar's
secret headquarters. One very tough customer.
Ex-green beret. Former Navy SEAL. Ran the
counter-terrorist division of the CIA. A some-
times special....

SMARTY
How come you're the one playing with the
computer; I'm the computer expert!

XYLENE
It's my compooter!

SMARTY
Fine. But it's my coffee! *(Takes coffee cup)*
Ha, ha ha ha. *(Walking away from him toward*
CYBORG WOMAN, notices her and protects
coffee) MINE!

JACKSON
But I thought Pike went to prison for high treason?

XYLENE
Quite right Mr. Jackson. Until a daring a prison
escape five years ago, which... *(Plays with*
computer but the screen goes blank. Embarrassed
and covering)...I don't have time to show you now.

SMARTY
Aww. I want to see the daring prison escape.

HARDGOD
SHUT UP!

SMARTY
Alright, alright. I'm feeling a lot of macroaggression here.

HARDGOD
So we've seen what we're up against. But I'm not sure your plan is gonna to work. I mean, splitting us up like this?

SMARTY
Yeah. *(Referring to KUNG FU GUY)* I mean what's an old guy like this supposed to do by himself? I mean, he's so old, he knew the Great Wall when it was just OK.

(SMARTY cracks up at his joke. No one thinks it's funny. KUNG FU GUY snaps his fingers, and SMARTY starts clucking like a chicken. KUNG FU GUY snaps his fingers again and SMARTY returns to normal)

XYLENE
If we don't trust each other and work as a team, the plan will fail. Take an example with Officer Jackson. He's always worked with a partner.

SMARTY
Yeah, and he's always gotten 'em killed.

JACKSON
What did you say, you fat turd?

HARDGOD
And what are you thinking sending some Robot Chick in to take out the security system? That is clearly man's work!

CYBORG WOMAN
Why? Does the job require you stick a cock in it?

HARDGOD
That's right! You just keep it up with your lip, woman!

CYBORG WOMAN
You're old and fat, and I could snap you like an old fat twig.

(They stare each other down, tension mounts. Suddenly they kiss passionately)

SMARTY
Now that is what I call a stupid cliché.

JACKSON
A fat, wise-cracking computer expert is also a stupid cliché.

SMARTY
Yeah, AH haa ...

(They stare each other down, tension mounts. Suddenly SMARTY kisses him passionately)

JACKSON
What the hell are you doing?

SMARTY
Just going with the flow.

(The team's bickering intensifies, but is silenced by KUNG FU GUY's powerful kung fu shriek. He has his samurai sword drawn and takes a swipe at a candle, all we hear is wind. He approaches the candle and it falls into six neatly cut pieces)

KUNG FU GUY
Six pieces, useless. *(Pulls a new, lit candle out)* One makes light.

(Gong)

SMARTY
Well, I wouldn't call them useless exactly, I mean you could always make votive candles out of them or something, and where did you get that new candle anyway?

HARDGOD
SHUT UP!

SMARTY
All right, all right.

HARDGOD
The old man is right. World Merge happens in less than 24 hours. It's time to boogie.

("BOOGIE MAN" plays as the TEAM struts their stuff to the airplane in slo-mo. XYLENE falls over backward in his wheelchair and the action stops)

XYLENE
A little help here.

(JACKSON and HARDGOD help him up)

XYLENE
I'm all right! I have no feelings in my legs anyway.

SMARTY
HA! That's lucky. *(Noticing his comment has tanked, he covers by starting to slo-mo walk all by himself, singing out of the side of his mouth)* I'm your boogie man, boogie man, that's what I am *(with an elbow to KUNG FU GUY)* help me out here.

XYLENE
Now that we've boogied to the plane, it's time to fly to Kreegar's secret headquarters in *(spits)* Florida.

(Organ fugue. Fade to black. Transition to:)

THE LOBBY OF KREEGAR'S SECRET HQ

HARDGOD
We're in! That was easy.

CYBORG WOMAN
That was just the front door!

HARDGOD
I know.

XYLENE
The hard part's ahead of us. Remember—once we reach sub-level one, Cyborg Woman will have 60 seconds to shut down the first Automated Security System. Most importantly, we want as little gun fire as possible. Shhhhtealth is the key to this mission.

(JACKSON and HARDGOD have been checking their guns and ammo when HARDGOD's gun goes off and gives every one a fright)

HARDGOD
(As if they're bent out of shape over nothing)
SORRY!

XYLENE
I'll be in constant communication with you at all times...

SMARTY
(Trying out his headset by touching a finger to his

ear) Left nut to squirrel, left nut to squirrel, are you receiving me?

XYLENE
...which should be a real joy! Jackson, are you ready for your distraction?

(JACKSON produces a mysterious paper bag, which he pats fondly, and winks knowingly)

XYLENE
All right. Let's go!

(All move out. Transition to GUARDs sitting around in a circle playing cards. GUARD 1 is not playing)

HEAD GUARD
This game is called five card *(insert funny phrase of the day)*, Queens are wild, Jokers are good for Aces, straights, and flushes...ante is six cents.

GUARD 1
(Looking over HEAD GUARD's shoulder) Are four Jacks good?

ALL
I'm out.

(One SLOW GUARD is still deciding. Slow burn)

SLOW GUARD
(Triumphantly slapping down a card) UNO, moth-erfuckers!

(Sinister music. JACKSON enters holding the head-shot of whoever plays KREEGAR with eyeholes cut out. This is his "Diversion")

JACKSON
(Pretending to be KREEGAR) All right, men.
Back to work.

(Nothing)

JACKSON
Chop chop.

(Nothing)

JACKSON
Time is money. *(Looks around the headshot to see
how is plan is working, then ducks back behind
headshot)* I'll be in my office. *(Exits, pursued by
guards)*

*(Music Cue: ominous music. HARDGOD and
SMARTY rush on. HARDGOD takes out two
Guards; another GUARD is pummeling SMARTY.
CYBORG WOMAN rushes the middle of the fray
on her way to Security Station One. HARDGOD
comes to the aid of SMARTY. SMARTY drags a
guard off stage, trying to remove his clothes)*

HARDGOD
Team one down, heading to team two!

*(CYBORG WOMAN has reached the first Security
section. She is wearing a metallic strap-on, which she
thrusts into the security station, shutting it down)*

CYBORG WOMAN
System one down.

XYLENE
(On head set) Good. You have one minute to
shut down the second system. Kung Fu Guy,
report.

(KUNG FU GUY appears, calmly ripping out the spine of a guard)

KUNG FU GUY
Merely waiting.

(Gong)

(JACKSON and HARDGOD enter from two different directions, fighting across two different areas. CYBORG WOMAN runs through the middle)

XYLENE
Hardgod, report on Team 2.

HARDGOD
Better get a Wet Vac—there's gonna be guts on the ceiling.

(CYBORG WOMAN rushes on and sticks her cock-like device into the security system)

CYBORG WOMAN
System 2 down.

XYLENE
You have three minutes to shut down the final system. It's on the far north end of sub-level three.

CYBORG WOMAN
Right.

(Meanwhile, SMARTY has entered, trying to put on a guard uniform that is way too small)

XYLENE
Alec.

SMARTY
Who's that?

XYLENE
DR. XYLENE!

SMARTY
Oh. What are you wearing?

XYLENE
Well, I have on a little.... *(angry sputter)* Proceed
to computer processing!

SMARTY
I'm on my way!

(A SCANTILY CLAD GUARD enters)

GUARD
Hey! Some guy just took my clothes!

SMARTY
That's a bummer.

*(They go to exit, pause, wonder, then split.
JACKSON and HARDGOD enter from either
end of a hallway, each fighting a guard. They each
grab their guard, and give a running headbutt into
each other, turn around, high five and continue
running off as CYBORG WOMAN runs through
the middle of it. SMARTY is hanging above a
terminal, Mission Impossible style, not 4 feet from
XYLENE's position on stage. He presses a button)*

SMARTY
I'm in the system.

XYLENE
I can't hear you. You're breaking up.

*(SMARTY walks over to XYLENE and talks
directly to him)*

SMARTY
I'm in the system.

XYLENE
We need you to find whose thumbprint opens the final security door.

SMARTY
All right. *(Pats XYLENE on the shoulder)*

XYLENE
Now remember—it changes every week, so don't be fooled by old records. *(Pause)* Have you found it yet?

SMARTY
No. It's like trying to find a handicapped parking space at the Special Olympics. Wait a minute! Here it is—Bradley Rivers, Chief Legal Advisor.

XYLENE
Kung Fu Guy. You got that?

KUNG FU GUY
Hi.

(BRADLEY and BRADLEY'S GOLFING BUDDY enter)

BRADLEY
So, I was taking my new Beemer out for a little test drive, and this bum tries to wash my windshield for FOOD! So I stuck him with my tazer! HA HA HA! ZOT! ZOT!

(The SCANTILY CLAD GUARD runs in)

GUARD
Uh, excuse...

BRADLEY
What what whatwhatwhatwhatwhat what WHAT!?

GUARD
A guy took my clothes, and I can't...

BRADLEY
Really? So what do you want me to do about
it, Nancy Boy? Go. Go. Gogogogogogogo GO!
(Chases the GUARD out) Now. Where was I?
Oh, yeah, so this bum is writhing around on the
ground in agony...

*(KUNG FU GUY, using his ninja magic, steals
BRADLEY's thumb)*

BRADLEY
...so I had my chauffeur kick him! Haha. Gimmie
a thumbs-up, baby!

*(Each gives a thumbs-up, but BRADLEY has no
thumb)*

GOLFING BUDDY
Where's yours?

BRADLEY
What the...?

(Funny bits involving looking for the thumb)

BRADLEY
Screw it, I'll buy me a new one. Yeah!

*(HARDGOD and JACKSON fighting in two
different areas. CYBORG WOMAN runs through.
HARDGOD takes out his opponent with karate)*

HARDGOD
KARATE!

JACKSON
Hardgod, where are you?

HARDGOD
One room south of you.

JACKSON
I've got a little present for you.

(JACKSON throws his opponent off stage left, a double flies on from stage right to HARDGOD. HARDGOD breaks the guard's arm, throws him back stage right, the original guard appears stage left with a broken arm and he runs past JACKSON)

HARDGOD
Aww, Jackson. You shouldn't have.

JACKSON
No sweat.

(CYBORG WOMAN shoves her cock-like device into the final security machine)

CYBORG WOMAN
Final system down.

XYLENE
Kung Fu Guy—do you have the thumb?

KUNG FU GUY
(Producing thumb) Hi.

XYLENE
Everyone rendezvous outside Kreegar's office. When you get there, the lead walls will cut off my communication, so good luck.

TEAM
Check!

KUNG FU GUY
Hi.

(Team runs off, except KUNG FU GUY, who turns downstage, thus "entering", then SMARTY, JACKSON, HARDGOD, and CYBORG WOMAN run on)

SMARTY
WE MADE IT!!

HARDGOD
Where's the thumb?

(KUNG FU GUY produces the thumb)

SMARTY
Hey. If that's the thumb, then who's thumb is this?

(SMARTY produces a novelty box with his thumb sticking out. He wiggles it, screams, then shows his other thumb, covered with a huge novelty thumb. More screaming, which peters off into giggles, then nothing. Noting that no one is laughing, he turns to CYBORG WOMAN)

SMARTY
You see this is a novelty thumb, and this is my real...

(CYBORG WOMAN smacks his hand into his face. KUNG FU GUY puts the severed thumb to the door, which opens)

HARDGOD
Ready? 1...2...3!

(The team storms in and is immediately surrounded by PIKE, POISON, and GUARDS. GUARDS

disperse, and the chair at the desk turns around, revealing...)

KREEGAR
Helllllooooo! Hardgod, you old so-and-so. Tell me—how are you? I mean really, how are you, you old hoody-hoo-and-the-hey-hey-nonny-nonny? Oh, and lookie look look – the gang's all here. I see you brought Cyborg Woman. Everything back in the right places, I trust, hmm? Hey, there's Kung Fu Guy. HI! How are you? Oh, and who brought Jimmy Buffet? Or should I say "buffét?" Well, welcome, welcome, welcome one and all, just the same, to my secret headquarters located...several feet below the surface of the Florida Everglades.

(Fish swim past the window)

HARDGOD
How many feet?

KREEGAR
That's several.

HARDGOD
Don't you mean ten?

KREEGAR
That's just the top! The bottom is located well over forty-two feet below the surface of the Florida Everglades! But I mustn't allow myself to be flustered by your petty wise-acring, for now is the time for gloating. *(Glides over his desk)* Nyah,Nyah, you lose, nanner, nanner, neener! I caught you! You got caught! Time for a little GLOAT DANCE. *(Begins to dance)*

CYBORG WOMAN
But how did you know—

KREEGAR
Whoa whoa whoa. Just a minute, I'm dancing here! So Rude! *(Finishes his dance then quickly composes himself)* You were saying?

CYBORG WOMAN
But how did you know we were coming?

KREEGAR
Oh, yeah, you see, it's quite simple, really. *(Pulls himself over the desk)* You see, we had someone on the inside.

(KREEGAR spins around, and two FRENCH ARTISTS enter with brushes and palettes and begin working on KREEGAR's face)

ARTIST 1
Bon soir, mon frérè.

ARTIST 2
Bon soir, monsieur. *(Pretentious voilà kiss. Exeunt FRENCH ARTISTS)*

KREEGAR
And his name…

(KREEGAR spins around, and he looks just like DR. XYLENE)

KREEGAR/XYLENE
…is ME!

(Stinger)

HARDGOD
Dr. Xylene! You betrayed us to Kreegar?

XYLENE
I *AM* KREEGAR!

(Stinger)

JACKSON
You mean all those times you used a handicapped parking space, you could have just as easily—

CYBORG WOMAN
(Pushing Jackson aside) But why? Why set up a team to take yourself out?

KREEGAR/XYLENE
If you throw a frog into boiling water, why, he'll jump right out. But if you slowly boil the water, and then throw him in... it's more calculating. HAHAHAH! You see, I need to sort out those who would even dare to oppose me, and eliminate them.

SMARTY
And our little plan worked, my friend.

(Stinger)

SMARTY
Just look at them. The trusting fools. I'll be upstairs.

KREEGAR/XYLENE
Shut up! You were never working for me.

SMARTY
(Through angry tears) Only because you never asked. I just hope Kreegar's bodyguard doesn't, oh, squash my head between her powerful thighs (hint, hint).

(POISON kicks him in the groin)

KREEGAR/XYLENE
Leave the lady killing... *(takes a gun from POISON and points it at CYBORG WOMAN)* ...to me.

HARDGOD
(An amazing discovery) You were wearing makeup!

KREEGAR/XYLENE
You see? You see why I want to kill him so much? Oh, Hardgod? Over here. Do you remember when I said I'd kill you last?

HARDGOD
No.

KREEGAR/XYLENE
Oh. I guess I never did say that, did I? Oh, well, time to die!

(GIRL SCOUT enters)

GIRL SCOUT
Would anyone like to buy some Girl Scout cookies?

HARDGOD
Cookies! Kreegar, I'm sure if we discussed this reasonably over a delicious Thin Mint Cookie, we could AHHHHHHHHHHHHHHHHHHHHHHHHHH!

(HARDGOD grabs the GIRL SCOUT and uses her to break the window. Blackout. Water rushes in. Lights up. The room is full of water. Enter an alligator. Alligator fight! Team and KREEGAR's men battle the alligator. Kokens blow bubbles at strategic times. Eventually, KUNG FU GUY uses Kung Fu Magic to hypnotize the gator before entering it and cutting it in half from the inside. KUNG FU GUY strikes a triumphant mie pose, but the dying alliga-

tor manages to bite him and the tail slaps him hard. HARDGOD pulls him out of the water. Transition to the surface. Much coughing. HARDGOD lays down the limp body of KUNG FU GUY)

HARDGOD
You're gonna be OK old man. You're gonna be OK.

KUNG FU GUY
No.

(He reveals his badly bitten torso. All gasp)

KUNG FU GUY
Now let me die with dignity.

SMARTY
Quick! Give him acupuncture! *(Plunges a retractable pen into the wound and starts clicking)* Am I doing this right?

(KUNG FU GUY snatches the pen and flicks it away)

KUNG FU GUY
Not effective. Today is a good day to die.

(Sad moment)

SMARTY
Isn't that more of a Native American thing to say?

ALL
SHUT UP!

SMARTY
God forbid someone here tries to culturally sensitive!

(KUNG FU GUY collapses. Good times montage. A series of silent images in slo-mo showing what "good times" the team has shared. Music Cue: the slow intro to "Everybody Was Kung Fu Fighting" on a loop. The montage is as follows:

—The team (HARDGOD, CYBORG WOMAN, ALEC, JACKSON, XYLENE and KUNG FU GUY) enjoys a summer day by flying a kite. Kung Fu Guy offers the string to Xylene. Xylene takes the kite and its wind power sends him wheeling off out of control. The team laughs good-naturedly at the handicapible hijinks.

—Next, the team is enjoying a day of fishing. Kung Fu Guy uses kung fu magic to make a fish fly into his hand and enjoys a bite of sushi. All laugh.

—Next, the team is playing a friendly game of 'spin the bottle'. Kung Fu Guy holds up the bottle for it is his turn to spin. He spins and whomever it lands on that night is treated to a kung fu guy kiss as all laugh.

—Next, the team is egging on Jackson and Kung Fu Guy in a beer chugging contest. Kung Fu Guy wins easily. All cheer and laugh.

—Next, the team is relaxing and Kung Fu Guy is reading what appears to be the Tao Te Ching. Alec is sneaking up on him with the "Sh!" gesture. He snatches the book away to reveal he is reading "Playboy". All laugh at Kung Fu Guy as Alec makes the humpy humpy gesture.

—Next, all the team is getting high on their various chosen drugs. Alec finishes off his nitrous balloon and goes to Kung Fu Guy and makes the humpy

humpy gesture. All are confused.

—*Finally, Kung Fu Guy is preparing for sleep as the team enters laughing. They notice Kung Fu Guy and quiet down, tucking him in with a blankie for a good nights sleep. They assume the same positions from before the montage)*

CHORUS
(Sad and slow) Everybody was kung fu fighting...

(The blankie disappears and we are now in the present)

HARDGOD
KUNG FU GUY! NOOOOOOOOOOOOOOO!
Let's get Kreegar! *(Callously drops the body, screams and runs off)*

SMARTY
Do we even know where Kreegar is?

CYBORG WOMAN
(Calmly) No.

(JACKSON and CYBORG WOMAN scream and run off)

SMARTY
Let's see. If I'm going to find Kreegar, I need to think like Kreegar. *(SMARTY improvises as KREEGAR, then suddenly—)* He's buying trans friendly pornography and inexpensive snack food items! Nope, I'm still thinking like me. But to be on the safe side, I better check the adult snack shop. *(Exits)*

(An open room. CYBORG WOMAN sweeps it, clear, lays gun aside and produces her diary and lays belly down on floor, kicking her legs back and forth)

CYBORG WOMAN
(In little girly voice) Dear Diary, I think Stone
Hardgod is dreamy. Do you think he notices me?

(POISON enters and steps on the diary)

CYBORG WOMAN
Poison, you bitch. How much did you hear?

POISON
Everything. I wish I was Stone Hardgod. Well,
except for the dick thing, and his back fat.

CYBORG WOMAN
His back's not fat. It's rugged.

POISON
Like two miles of bad road!

CYBORG WOMAN
That tears it. *(Grabs a quarterstaff)*

POISON
Oh, you want to fight with those? How Freudian.
Am I sensing a little penis envy?

CYBORG WOMAN
Shall we throw doughnuts at each other instead?

(POISON grabs her quarterstaff. Fight)

POISON
Join me Cyborg Woman, and together we'll go
further and further across the line that separates
warm flesh and cold steel.

CYBORG WOMAN
Give it up Poison, I only have eyes for men.
Well, except for my roommate freshmen year of
college—you know, it was an experimental time—
and she had the cutest little nose ring.

POISON
Did you make any videos?

CYBORG WOMAN
What's left of my flesh is crawling. *(CYBORG WOMAN proceeds to thrash and then kill POISON)* Stay...out...of...MY...diary! *(Snaps POISON's neck)*

POISON
You could have said "killing you would be a snap!" *(Dies)*

CYBORG WOMAN
(Picking up her diary) Now I know how Anne Frank feels. *(Exits)*

(Transition to corridor with HARDGOD at Door #1. A single door is used over and over to kick open. He kicks it open. Sound of a woman screaming in the shower)

HARDGOD
Sorry.

(Kicks down Door #2. Sound of a man saying, "oh yeah" and a cow mooing)

HARDGOD
Sorry...

(Kicks down Door #3. Unloads his clip. Looks into room)

HARDGOD
Sorry.

(Kicks down Door #4. The door exits as HARDGOD enters the store room. Lockers and a Webber grill and a copy machine and big electri-

cal box that reads "Danger!" HARDGOD sweeps the room and opens a locker door and a cat jumps onto his face. He wrestles with it, throws. A gun shot hits the cat midair. HARDGOD is confused. PIKE enters from locker holding a large gun)

PIKE
I see you've met my cat!

(They exchange gunfire, reload and both akido roll into standing positions, guns leveled at the temples. Click. Click. Both come up empty. Huge fight involving a ladder, a quarterstaff and whatever else comes in handy. After much fighting, HARDGOD breaks PIKE's arm. He smashes PIKE in the face with a street sign. HARDGOD shoves PIKE'S arm into the electrical box)

HARDGOD
Shocking isn't it? *(Puts a chef's hat on PIKE's head and shoves PIKE's face into the grill)* Hot enough for ya?

(HARDGOD breaks the glass on the copier with PIKE's face. The copier spits out copies of the actor playing PIKE's headshot. HARDGOD sets one aflame and lights a cigar)

HARDGOD
You'll never reproduce.

(Enter JACKSON, CYBORG, and SMARTY)

JACKSON
Hardgod! Hurry! Kreegar's leaving!

CYBORG WOMAN
On a jet plane!

SMARTY
And I don't know when he'll be coming back
again!

HARDGOD
Let's go!

*(All run off screaming. A world map shows the
voyage to the North Pole to cover the transition to:)*

AIRPLANE WING

*(Lights up on an airplane wing with our four heroes
hanging from it)*

KREEGAR
(Opening the door to the plane) Helloooooo!
Welcome aboard "KreegAir", Flight 666, flying
non-stop...to your DOOOOOM!

*(Stinger. Spotlight. KREEGAR rushes down the
wing to stand in the spotlight and then rushes
back)*

KREEGAR
It's too late to stop me. In fifteen minutes, the
"Harmonic Discordance" occurs. At that timeless
instant, I shall be at the North—*(pointing toward
the tail of the plane)*—no, wait, North—*(pointing
in the direction the plane is heading)* Pole, where
I will place the Paperweight of Syfan upon the
Loose Papers of Eldrich, thus summoning Syfan
the Eldrich, who will suck up all the souls of the
world and give their power to me.

SMARTY
Then you might finally be able to get it up? Huh?
Get it up?

KREEGAR

Well, Mr. Alec Smarty, your name certainly reflects your demeanor. Perhaps now you should change your name to... Justin Shit. YEAH! SUPER-BURN! Tell me, are you a gambling man, Mr. Smarty?

SMARTY

Well, I once played Strip Poker with your mother.

JACKSON, HARDGOD, CYBORG WOMAN

Who hasn't?

KREEGAR

Oh, that is so mature—you guys don't even know my mom! *(Kicks CYBORG off of the plane)*

HARDGOD

Cyborg Woman! NOOOOOOOOOOOOOOO! *(Releases his grip and goes after her)*

SMARTY

(Looking coyly to JACKSON) If I let go, will you try to save me? *(Smiles seductively)* Oops! *(He lets go and flies off)*

JACKSON

(Looking back) No.

KREEGAR

Man, I thought he'd never leave. Now that we're alone, I have a confession to make. I can tell by the way you use your walk, you're a woman's man. *(JACKSON attempts to say something, and KREEGAR gives him the "Don't Speak!" gesture)* No time to talk! Therefore, I will allow you to die with your dignity.

(Dealer's choice. KREEGAR does something to

destroy all his dignity, like quickly put a rainbow afro wig on JACKSON, spray him with seltzer, and moon him. Your choice)

KREEGAR
(Chicken walking on the plane wing in victory)
Chicken walking all around the wing on that one, baby! Yeah!

(After finishing his chicken walk, KREEGAR stomps JACKSON's hands and sends him flying as well. He looks around, self-satisfied)

KREEGAR
Who's flying the plane? Ooh! *(Rushes back into the plane. Transition to:)*

THE NORTH POLE

(The TEAM runs on, brushing themselves off from the long fall)

HARDGOD
According to this compass, every direction is south, so we must be here.

CYBORG WOMAN
Let me see that. That's not a compass! It's a chocolate coin!

(She throws it. SMARTY races after the precious chocolate coin, but is stopped by...)

KREEGAR
Helloooo! Just in time to see the end of the world. Thirty seconds to Harmonic Discordance.

HARDGOD
Wrong. Thirty seconds to tear you a third asshole!

(They shoot wildly and lots of bullets, all of which seem to hurt KREEGAR at first, but we see no blood)

KREEGAR
Don't shoot! I'm mortally wounded! Ouch, Ouch....

(The bullets are doing no apparent damage, so HARDGOD rushes KREEGAR and meets an invisible force field. SMARTY pokes the force field)

KREEGAR
Super burn. Sticks and stones may break my bones, but not within my magic protective gobo!

(Chimes strike midnight)

KREEGAR
(Looks at his watch) Times up! *(Evil laugh)*

(All move towards him in slow motion "NO!"... Lights dim and there is a burst of radiant energy as SYFAN, a 12 foot tall puppet walks on and tears KREEGAR's head off, drop kicks it, does a victory jig and exits)

KREEGAR
I've been beheaded! How is it I'm able to speak?

(Kreegar's beheaded body wanders off. Everyone is unconscious, HARDGOD comes to and rushes to CYBORG WOMAN)

HARDGOD
Cyborg Woman! Nooooooooooooooooooooo! First I won the girl, then I lost the girl...

CYBORG WOMAN
(Coming to) Hardgod?

HARDGOD
Then I won the girl again!

CYBORG WOMAN
Hardgod, you big dumb ox!

(Music Cue: Love song. HARDGOD and CYBORG WOMAN kiss while ALEC and JACKSON look on. JACKSON notices a Loose Paper of Eldrich and reads)

JACKSON
Well, looks like Kreegar's plan failed because he had no love.

HARDGOD
Ah, love. The missing ingredient.

(SMARTY looks at JACKSON who is smiling and plants a big, fat, sloppy one on him)

JACKSON
(Pushing him away) I wish you would knock that off!

SMARTY
Sorry.

(SMARTY is walking off dejected and pathetic, JACKSON looks on and feels like a great big heel, walks over to SMARTY and takes him by the shoulders)

JACKSON
I'm a liar.

(They kiss passionately, finally able to utter the love that dares not speak its name. The angel of KUNG FU GUY appears and bows, nodding his approval)

SMARTY
I almost forgot to tell you guys! I've rigged this place to blow in about 10 seconds!

(They all react then freeze like an old school TV episode, except for SMARTY who continues)

SMARTY
I'm not kidding!

(They all unfreeze, look at him, and collectively realize that he isn't kidding. They all run. LOUD EXPLOSION. Blackout)

THE END?

ABOUT THE PLAYWRIGHTS

Joe Foust is a sexy beast. As Nick Offerman said about Joe on LATE NIGHT WITH DAVID LETTERMAN, "When I saw him, I said to myself, 'I wanna hang with this guy. He knows just the kind of trouble I want to get into.'" A writer, actor, director, and fight director based in Chicago, Joe has acted at The Goodman, Steppenwolf, Wisdom Bridge, Remy Bumppo, Next, TheaterWit, Court, Chicago Shakespeare Theatre, First Folio, Penninsula Players, Cleveland Playhouse, Syracuse Stage, New Victory on Broadway, Maltz Jupiter, Milwaukee Shakespeare and is a founding member of Defiant Theater, where his credits include directing and either writing or co-writing ACTION MOVIE: THE PLAY, SCI-FI ACTION MOVIE IN SPACE PRISON, HORROR MOVIE: THE PLAY, and UBU RAW. He recently wrote Robin Hood play with John Maclay, and they are presently collaborating on two more.

◊   ◊   ◊

Husband, father, writer, director, mystery man, and science hero, **Richard Ragsdale** keeps busy. A founding member of Chicago's Defiant Theatre, Richard wrote, directed, or acted in a majority of the plays presented by that august body. As a founder and teacher at Ham Club, a group that teaches theatre and puts on plays with public schools, Richard takes great delight in passing on his love of theatre in general and shtick and clowning in particular to a new generation of stage nerds. He likes horror movies, Disneyland, and embroidery, and thinks everyone looks better in a cape.

MORE FROM SORDELET INK

PLAYSCRIPTS

WWW.SORDELETINK.COM

SORDELET INK BOOKS BY DAVID BLIXT

NELLIE BLY
WHAT GIRLS ARE GOOD FOR
CHARITY GIRL
CLEVER GIRL

THE STAR-CROSS'D SERIES
THE MASTER OF VERONA
VOICE OF THE FALCONER
FORTUNE'S FOOL
THE PRINCE'S DOOM
VARNISH'D FACES: STAR-CROSS'D SHORT STORIES

WILL & KIT
HER MAJESTY'S WILL

THE COLOSSUS SERIES
COLOSSUS: STONE & STEEL
COLOSSUS: THE FOUR EMPERORS

EVE OF IDES - A PLAY

NON-FICTION
SHAKESPEARE'S SECRETS: ROMEO & JULIET
TOMORROW, AND TOMORROW: ESSAYS ON MACBETH
FIGHTING WORDS

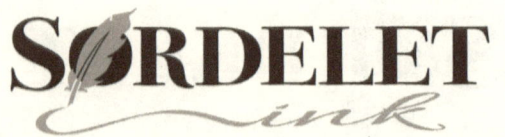

www.ingramcontent.com/pod-product-compliance
Lightning Source LLC
Chambersburg PA
CBHW020641130626
46552CB00003B/1343